KRISHNA IS MY WORLD

VIJAY GOMATHINAYAGAM

Contents

CHAPTER I

Aaliyah, Krishna and Vincent

Aaliyah, the name is known to the whole world. She is the founder of the company "Aanya", an artificial intelligence company, headquartered at Mumbai, invented a bot which achieved a 78% in the turing test(human test for artificial intelligence), the score which is not reached by any other artificial intelligence bot. She is just 25 and she is the richest person in the world. She has ten times more money than the world's second richest person. Her bot is used in every smart device. From smartphones, computers to smart rings.

She has a best friend Gargi, from School. She would have married Gargi, if Gargi is a man and not a woman. She would share everything with her friend Gargi. Gargi works as a technical support in an IT company.

Aaliyah and Gargi would meet up every saturday night in their favourite ice cream shop in Hanuman nagar, Mumbai. As today is Saturday, March 1, Aaliyah came to the shop in her Bugatti. The shopkeeper would reserve all the tables at the same time every Saturday, the time when Aaliyah and Gargi would meet. Aaliyah's z plus security team would make sure that the crowd will not come closer to Aaliyah for selfies and there is no threat to Aaliyah's life. People will look in disbelief, how a world's richest person could come to such a small ice cream shop. People will take photos of Aliyah, her car, her security etc. Shopkeeper, the same person who sometimes offered ice cream for free in Aaliyah's school time, is ready to serve two chocobar ice creams to Aaliyah and Gargi. They met and got their order served. As they started savouring, Aaliyah asked Gargi "how was your week?", Gargi told Aaliyah about a new employee Krishna, who has recently joined her team. She said, "he looks to be introverted, and reserved. I seriously wonder why anyone would hire an introvert for support work". Aaliyah said, "introverts are mostly intelligent, most of my employees are introverts. They get their job done". Gargi then asked Aaliyah, "how was your week?". Aaliyah replied, "as usual, looking after my company, board meetings etc". "Actually I had a hibiscus plant which I left without watering for more than 2 weeks, some of its branches were spoiled with fungus disease. I removed those branches, watered the plant daily for 5 days, and now the plant looks fresh and beautiful. I got really happy, the happiness which I never felt possessing luxurious materials, driving 1500 horsepower car which reaches from 0 to 60 miles in just 2.3 seconds, getting signature massages, savouring dishes prepared by world's greatest chef, yachting, driving a vintage car, casino, wearing designer dresses, dating a super hot model, more than anything else in the world". "I found that we get real happiness by bettering the life of other living things, it can be a plant, a human or animal". Gargi replied "giving is better than receiving", "the good thing is, anyone in the world can experience this happiness". Aaliyah said "exactly, even winding my mechanical watch gives me happiness". Gargi smiled and said, "I can understand why the founder of a successful AI company is not wearing a smartwatch". Aaliyah smiled and said "people always run behind money but they do not know that the money does not give them the satisfaction they are longing for". Aaliyah waved to her assistant to pay the bill and said "bye Gargi, we can meet up next Saturday next chocobar". Gargi replied "bye, I will pay the bill next time.". "Sure" said Aaliyah

Aaliyah was invited to the women empowerment program, which was conducted by the company where Gargi works and Aaliyah does not want to disclose it to Gargi, as the company also wants to keep it as a secret to surprise their employees. On March 8, international women's day, Aaliyah and four other women CEOs were received by the company. Gargi did not expect Aaliyah would make time for this program and she was really happy seeing her face. Gargi was jumping from the ground to the sky in excitement. All five women were made to sit on a round sofa with great honour. As a welcome gift, beautiful flower bouquets were to be given to all five women by the company's new employee Krishna. When Aaliyah received the flower bouquet, she noticed how neatly dressed he was, he did not wear any costly dress or expensive watch or shoes. His dress was the most modest than any other employee's dress but it was neatly ironed, green color shirt was perfectly tucked, belt buckle was neatly aligned with his black pant and shirt button, black tie was pinned with silver color pin to the shirt properly, properly polished black shoes, his hair was neatly combed, his beard was clean shaven, and also he smelled good. For a split second, her heart told her that he is the man that she should be living with. Krishna asked her to look at the camera for the photo, she even liked his deep and confident voice. All five received their bouquet and they were discussing their achievements, struggles they faced and also they provided advice for the employees.

Aaliyah was also discussing the future plans of her company that she was planning to invent an AI feature that would identify the trash content in the social media websites as it would assure that people will be able to consume only good content and the challenges that they are facing to implement that feature, she says that they will be able to introduce this feature only after 2 years as it requires more effort. Krishna liked her idea as almost 80 percent of content found in social media is trash. Also, Krishna does not use any social media websites. Krishna was asked to direct those five women to the lunch hall. As Krishna approached those women and called them for lunch, he was looking at 4 other women except Aaliyah and his voice was a little shaky and it was not as confident as before. His fast beating heart was easily felt by Aaliyah. As they were walking, Gargi approached Aaliyah and praised for her speeches. Aaliyah asked Gargi, the name of the new employee who was walking before them. Gargi told her that he is the introverted guy Krishna that she mentioned yesterday. Gargi was curious as to why she wanted to know his name and she asked her why. Aaliyah replied that he is very simple. Gargi can sense that Aaliyah likes him but she does not want to discuss that now. They approached the guest lunch hall, Gargi told her that they will meet in the ice cream shop as today is Saturday and left. Aaliyah had a nice chat with the other four at lunch. Aaliyah was really happy that she attended this program. Aaliyah thanked the company representatives and left for her work.

That day, as usual Aaliyah and Gargi met in the ice cream shop. Gargi asked Aaliyah, "Do you like Krishna?". Aaliyah replied, "I think I am in love, I have never felt this kind of feeling before". Gargi asked, "Do you like him just because he is simple?". Aaliyah replied, "I don't know, the moment I saw him, some magic happened, I cannot come up with any reason". Gargi said, "I don't know whether he is single or not". Aaliyah said, "he is single". Gargi asked, "how can you be so sure?". Aaliyah said "I know, he was trying to be casual in front of me". Gargi said, "that means, he too likes you, just you two have to tell each other". Aaliyah said, "before that, I want you to speak to Krishna. Just ask him what he will do if I propose to him".   Aaliyah also asked, "whether Krishna knows that we are friends?". Gargi replied, "yes, my whole company knows. Tomorrow is Sunday, I will ask him on Monday". Aaliyah asked, "why don't you ask him tomorrow in a phone call? Conference call, just don't tell him that I am in the line". Gargi said, "ok, anything for you my dear". Gargi paid the bill and they left.

The next day, Gargi called Aaliyah, and Aaliyah picked the call. Gargi has put Aaliyah on hold. Gargi, then called Krishna, he picked the call. They are in conference now. Gargi asked whether he had taken any photos in the women's day celebration which happened the day before. Krishna replied, "yes", again his voice was confident. Aaliyah felt butterflies in her stomach. Krishna does not use any social media apps but he uses whatsapp, so Gargi asked him whether he could send them to her. Krishna said, "sure I will send you the photos". Gargi asked, "do you have photos of chief guests, I want to surprise my friend Aaliyah by putting instagram status". Krishna said, "I think I have it, yes I have some photos of all chief guests, photos of Aaliyah too.". The first time Aaliyah heard Krishna uttering her name. This time, the butterflies count is multiplied by 10. Gargi then asked, "can I ask you something by the time you select all the photos and send them?". Krishna replied "why not? yes". Gargi asked, "Do you think Aaliyah is beautiful?". Krishna replied, "Hmmm...she looks fair". Gargi asked, "fair?". Krishna replied, "yes fair but...honest". Gargi asked, "What will you do If my friend proposes to you?". Now Aaliyah's heart was beating fast. Krishna replied, "That will never happen. Even If I work my whole life, spend very reasonably and save all remaining money, The money will be less than her one second income". Gargi didn't know what to reply, she said, "just kidding", and asked "I think you have sent all the photos?". Krishna said, "yes". Gargi said, "thank you so much! Have a wonderful weekend, Bye". Krishna said, "You too! Bye". Krishna dropped from the call. Then Aaliyah said, "I will call you later, Bye". Gargi said "Bye".

Aaliyah decides to meet Krishna. Aaliyah reaches Krishna's apartment house that evening. Aaliyah rang Krishna's door bell. Krishna opened the door and he was shocked to meet Aaliyah. He cannot believe his eyes. Krishna can hear his own heart thumping love beats. He is looking at Aaliyah like he is looking at a female goddess. He feels like he is skydiving some 2000 feets above the ground. Aaliyah is looking at Krishna like she is looking at a rare gem that humankind has never seen before. Aaliyah can feel Krishna's love for her. They both were speechless for a few seconds. Aaliyah breaks the silence, asking Krishna, "May I come in". Krishna struggled to bring up his voice. He said, "please come in". Aaliyah asked her security to wait outside. The home was very small, around 250 square feet, one room, one small kitchen and a restroom. Krishna began to ask Aaliyah to sit on the sofa, "Aaliyah, please...". Aaliyah told Krishna, "I love you". Krishna felt that he was even happy to die at that moment. Krishna told Aaliyah, "Gargi actually asked what I would do if you proposed to me". Then Aaliyah immediately said, "Sorry, I was also in the line, that was a conference call, I requested Gargi to not tell you that it was a conference call". Although Krishna would lead a happiest life with Aaliyah, he will even carry her for his whole life, he will do whatever he can for Aaliyah, he does not even want to touch her and he will be happy just by serving her. But Krishna had two thoughts, one is that he wants to live his life with his own earnings and he does not want to live with others' money. Second is that Krishna thought Aaliyah's decision is not a thoughtful decision, a world's richest woman cannot be with a man who depends on monthly income. Krishna just wants Aaliyah to lead a happiest life. Krishna replied, "your face is not even registered in my mind, although I have seen news about you, read about you on the internet, I have seen you yesterday". Aaliyah replied immediately, "LIE". Aaliyah cannot understand why Krishna said this. Krishna said, "your life is different, my life is different, you will find a perfect pair, All the best!". Aaliyah did not want to argue with him. Aaliyah said, "I can see pure love in your eyes and that is more precious than anything else" and she left his home.

World's second richest man Vincent's spy watches Aaliyah leaving Krishna's apartment house from a nearby building. Vincent also runs a technology company that is not as good as Aaliyah's, not even close. As his spy informed him about this, he asked his hackers and detectives to collect details about Krishna who is living at that apartment house. They first collected Krishna's phone number from his apartment owner by frightening. They collected all details about Krishna, his native place, his family members, the company where he works, his employment details. They cannot find any social media accounts of Krishna. But hackers found some photos of him in Gargi's instagram account. They hacked Krishna's phone, tried to find the call recordings, but they could not find any. Then they hacked Gargi's phone, found call recordings. They listened to the conference call and got to know that Aaliyah is in love with Krishna. They informed Vincent about this. Vincent thought that he finally found a way to end Aaliyah's monopoly.

The next day when Krishna went to his office, his manager arranged a meeting with him. In that meeting, his manager told Krishna, "your performance is not meeting the team's expectation". Krishna tried to defend by saying, "But I have completed every task that I was provided on time". Then his manager pointed out a mistake that Krishna made and told him that because of that mistake their client got upset. Krishna told, "Yes, But I will make sure, that will not happen again". Krishna was so afraid because he depends on the salary for his expenses and also he sends a part of his income to his mother. His father died of a heart attack when he was just 20. He completed his studies by educational loan. He is 26 now and has 5 years experience. Krishna has a 7 years younger sister who is pursuing a B.Tech course in a college. His family is residing at Coimbatore, TamilNadu. His manager said bluntly, "you are not adding any value to the team, you are also wasting other resources' time", he also said, "our company has a good reputation, you should protect that whenever you speak to a client, because of you our company will lose the reputation. I do not know how you got selected to this company, even junior resources have more product knowledge than you, you are totally unfit for this job". Krishna thought to fight his manager by asking him to behave professionally, but he understood there is no use in fighting with him. Krishna finally accepted whatever his manager told him. Krishna received an email saying that, that day is the last working day and he wants to complete all no dues within that day. Krishna does not want to discuss this with anyone in his team as he has not shared any personal matters with them or listened to theirs. It's been only three weeks since he joined this team. Krishna does not even discuss this with Gargi until evening. Just before leaving the company, Krishna shared this with Gargi, Gargi was so angry about the manager's behavior but Krishna requested her not to react to this.

Krishna reached his home, he tried to wipe off everything that his manager told him from his mind and he decided to apply for jobs in other companies. Krishna got a call from an unknown number. Krishna answered the call,

Krishna: "Hello"

Unknown person: "Hi Krishna"

Krishna: "Who are you?"

Unknown person: "Not important. Do you have money for your expenses, you are also sending a part of your salary to your mom right? How are you going to manage?"

Krishna: "I have not shared this information with anyone, how do you know that?"

Unknown person: "again, not important, just do whatever I say, you will get a job and your family members will be safe, your sister will get a high paying job after her college"

Krishna: "Why do I want to do it? I will call the police"

Unknown person: "how did you lose your job, is it because of your performance? What would you do if your mom and sister died in a gas cylinder blast?"

Krishna: "Why are you doing this to me?"

Unknown person: "you are Aaliyah's love right? apply for software developer job postings in Aanya company and tell Gargi that you have applied to that company's job postings, we have our men everywhere, some employees of her company are working for us, do not ask me why and do not try to talk about this to anyone, even to Aaliyah, don't forget your family, Bye"

Krishna had no choice, he applied to the software developer job postings in Aanya company and he informed Gargi that he has applied for three job postings in Aanya company. Gargi asked Krishna, "how did you apply, since Aanya company does not have technical support jobs". Krishna told her that he also has 2 years experience as a software developer. Gargi wished him good luck for getting a job in that company. Then Gargi immediately called Aaliyah and she was also free, so she attended that call. Gargi told what happened to Krishna that she cannot believe and also told about his application in her company. Aaliyah told Gargi, "Krishna will never have to worry about anything, he will get a call tomorrow". Vincent was happy, as everything was happening as he planned. Krishna got a call from the unknown person. The unknown person asked him to ask for the "work from home" option for the first three months. Krishna said that he will ask that.

The next morning Krishna got a call from Aanya company's HR, asking for his availability for an interview. Krishna gave his available time and asked the HR that he wants the "work from home" option for the first three months. HR told him that she will call him again after confirming with the team. HR called him again and told him that he can avail that option.

It was just one virtual round. After that, he got a call from HR saying that he got selected and they sent an offer letter to his email, asking him to join the next day as discussed with him. The HR person told him that he will have to come to the office for the first day alone to meet his team, to collect his laptop, accessories, ID card and to complete the onboarding process.

Aaliyah felt like she had collected the rare gem and she did not want to lose it at any cost. Actually Vincent's thought was, in order to destroy a person, it is enough to destroy their name. Vincent cannot do anything directly to her, so he has to take this route. Vincent has many men to do these kinds of things, but they cannot do more harm than the person that Aaliyah loves. Vincent needs someone who is able to gaslight her constantly, damage her self image completely and turn her into a monster. Someone who has great potential like Aaliyah when they turn into a monster, they do more terrifying things that other people cannot even imagine. The people are celebrating Aaliyah, lifting her above their heads, he wants the same people to stamp her under their feet. He will be the world's richest person then.

That night, The unknown person tells Krishna to install a monitoring app in his smartphone which Krishna installs. Then, Krishna called his mother and said that he had switched the company. His mother got afraid and asked him whether he fought with anyone. Krishna told his mother that all the people who were working at that project had to leave the company because the company had suddenly decided to close the project and he asked her not to worry. Krishna said that the new company has offered him three months work from home. His mother was so happy hearing that. He told his mother that he will be catching the flight the next night and arriving home. Just 2 minutes after he hung his call, the unknown person sent him the flight tickets which Krishna did not expect.

The next day Krishna goes to Aanya company to complete his onboarding process. After entering the office, he likes whatever things he sees, from the security person at the gate to the tissues placed in the restroom. He meets the HR, he collects his ID card, laptop. He then meets the team. The team manager arranges a meeting for the team to welcome Krishna. Everyone introduces themselves to him, then he gives his self introduction. One person suddenly asked him, "what is the reason that you left your previous job within 3 weeks". Manager told that person not to ask such questions. Then the manager said, "Krishna will be working remotely for the first three months". Then the team asked him for the joining treat for which Krishna accepted. Everyone in the team was very kind and helpful to him. After the end of business hours, Krishna left the office and went to his home. Once he reached the home, just after closing the door, he got a call from an unknown person.

Unknown person said "well done, we have to train you for the first three months, when Gargi calls you, speak in an unexcited tone". Krishna said "ok".

He then received a call from Gargi. He attended the call. Gargi asked, "How was your first day at Aanya!". Krishna said, "it was good". Gargi then asked, "did you get a chance to speak with your team members?". Krishna said, "Sorry, I am moving to my hometown today, can I call you later". Gargi said, "Sure, Bye". Krishna said "Bye".

He boards the flight and reaches his hometown. At once his mother saw him, she got worried that he was not eating properly. He met his sister. His sister likes him more than anyone else in the world, she would do anything for him. He will do anything to make her happy. That night, Krishna cannot eat more than 2 chapatis. His mother and sister doubted whether he was thinking about something because they had not seen him like this. He looks like he is being haunted. Krishna tried his best to act normal. The unknown person's voice is continuously running in his mind.

From the next day, Krishna received many calls from the unknown person. Krishna will enter into his room whenever he receives the call. He would tell his mother that the call is from his colleagues. Aside from his company work, Krishna will be talking over the phone. First he was trained how to dress, how to style his hair, and how to speak in front of Aaliyah. Then he was also given training on how to give a great french kiss. Sometimes he even receives image and video explanations. Then they taught him all the code words that they would use to communicate with him so that even if someone sees they cannot understand those messages. They sent him a bluetooth neckband headset that he will be wearing whenever he is with Aaliyah. They told him that the headset should always be connected with the phone so that they can hear their conversations.

Then they trained him with the following psychological mind tricks that he has to follow each day.

He should never speak less of other people whenever he is with Aaliyah because that would make her more confident.

He should not show true emotions to her, importantly he should never get angry at her because he will look immature to Aaliyah.

When she shares any good memories from her past, he should make fun of that or make her feel that she should not have shared with him.

He should have a mocking smile on his face whenever she is not looking at him directly but he is in her view, and when she notices the mocking smile, he should act as though he is trying to hide his smile and make some pleasing conversation as though he is trying to divert her, this would make a person doubt their own sanity.

Whenever possible, he should compare some of her qualities to other girl's, he should make her feel that she should improve on those qualities, if possible compare her with the person that she knows, for example her friend Gargi.

He should make her feel that she is coming after him and he is trying to keep distance. This is one of the reasons why they asked him to request a three months "work from home" option. This is why he was asked to speak in an unexcited tone to Gargi.

If Aaliyah says something good about him or praises him or buys him any gift, he should never miss that opportunity, he should speak something bad about her or speak about her weakness immediately, because she feels more pain when she is hurted by a person she loves. Also, she should never get a feeling that she has done something good for him.

He should always challenge her in some ways, and she should be made to take up the challenges, she should try to win him. He should never give her the satisfaction of winning those challenges, this will increase her rage. This will increase the chance of her outburst. Little drops of water make a mighty ocean. This is the most important of all. Also, this will make her engage with him more than any other important work.

He should make her doubt that he has relations with other girls. This will damage the self image more.

He should always try to make her guilty, tell her that he cannot do something or missed something good or made a wrong decision because of her. Guilty persons are more vulnerable, they will be ready to accept abuse because of their guilt. He should speak ill of her whenever she is guilty.

If she tries to achieve something, he should immediately set an impossible goal or speak in a way that she will not be achieving that goal. She will have to lose hope in anything that she wants to achieve. By closing every other door but one, she will eventually enter into that door.

He should speak bad of her little by little to her relations. Mainly to her friend Gargi. Over time, even her friend should not be surprised when Aaliyah has actually done something mischievous. Everyone's mind around Aaliyah must be tuned accordingly.

Whatever mind trick he is performing with Aaliyah, he should do as though he is doing it for her improvement, when Aaliyah believes that, she will not doubt the most glaring trick that he performs and she will not find the true intentions. Also, overtime, he should tell her directly that he wants to improve her in some ways.

Whenever she overthinks about him and his actions. He should act as though he is concentrating on some other things, he can just sing a song, hum any tune. It makes her feel that she overthinks about something unnecessarily.

Wherever she feels like she gets offended, he should pity her, make her believe that he is helping her to get around. He will appear more superior than her and she will be dependent on him.

Whenever he is asking her to do something, he should speak in a way that he does not want her to make any mistakes. Subconsciously making her believe that she might make any mistakes in anything that she does.

If she ignores his calls for no reason, he should act as though he got upset and he should ask why she cannot attend the call. If she lies, he should speak to her sarcastically and if she tells the truth, he should advise her not to repeat. People like Aaliyah do not like advice, she will turn worse.

He should constantly speak about her mistakes, wrong decisions. Even if there is none currently, he should speak about things that happened in the past. Only a clear mind can make a correct decision.

He should forward all the messages that he receives from unknown person to her, mostly they are motivational messages or messages that will remind her weaknesses. It can be text messages or meme photos or videos. Motivational quotes make her feel weak, weakness the sole reason for violence.

He should provoke her always, remind her about the things for which she gets more emotional.

Since he installed the monitoring software in his smartphone, the unknown person will also be able to listen to phone calls parallelly, Krishna will be speaking through his headphone, so he will be able to see messages in phone, and he can speak to her as instructed.

Overtime, he should make her feel that she is worthless although she is the richest person in the world. In some situations, he will have to tell her directly.

Stress will make her eat more. He should encourage her to eat more sugar and fat. She has access to all exotic foods in the world. She should use food to regain the happy hormones and crave more entering into a vicious cycle.

Reverse psychology works best for persons like Aaliyah. When she needs to do something, he should ask her not to do that, it will increase the chance of her doing it.

If she tries to mock him back, he should not get offended, he should make her feel that whatever she has done is not enough. She will try something more and he should repeat the same. He should act that he is victorious in front of her. Ultimately, she will be like a monkey with fire in its tail in a forest.

He should always try to engage her in a cold war with him. Even if she is not doing that, he should make her think that she has actually done some actions to win over him in that cold war.

He should make her forget her work. He should take her to movies, beaches, parks etc.

He should always point out some mistakes in her diet, hairstyle, dressing sense, lifestyle routine.

Whenever she is guilty and not ready to apologize to him. He should tell her that she has never apologized to him for any of her mistakes, this makes her devilish.

Even if she loves him, she may not provide him full attention in their conversations somtimes. In order to get her full attention, he must speak something that she finds more pleasing to hear, then suddenly he should speak something ill of her that will give her more pain. Again, before she recovers from that, he should pity her and act as though he is trying to make her get around. He should give her the pain, then show her mercy for her weakness and he should repeat this cycle.

He should do whatever he can to make her look less superior. He will be taking more candid photos, posting those photos where he looks cool and she does not. If she is alone in the photo, he should add some filters to make her think that he has done editing in order to make that photo look good.

Whenever she does something that she herself feels good about, he should do something greater than that. She should not develop a good relationship with him.

Whenever she is going to complete something big, just before she completes, he should ask whether that is completed. She should never get the satisfaction from the completion of that work.

Overtime, after making her guilty for many times, he should speak to her in a disgusting and authoritative tone, he should look at her disgustingly.

He should give her the feeling that he is just using her for his needs.

He should make her do some petty things.

She might find that he is not doing these things by himself. She might also ask him whether someone is asking him to do such things or She might try to talk about the indirect abuse that he does to her. At any cost, he should not tell the truth, he should act as though he cannot understand what she is asking.

Whenever she feels low, he should make her do something which she finds very easy to do or something which she is talented to do or something that she recently learned to do that will make her feel weak.

He should not always abuse her and he should not always be nice to her. When she is happy he should abuse, when she is very low he should be nice.

Whatever action she takes, she should be afraid whether that would go wrong.

When she makes the first move for sex, he should act as though he is trying to neglect her, increasing her rage.

After some days, he will have to speak about all psychological issues like anxiety, depression, PTSD, ADHD, personality disorders, OCD, panic attack. She should doubt herself whether she has some issues. He should not tell her directly that she has some psychological issue, instead he should tell her that he is affected by several problems and that is because of her.

After training Krishna with these mind tricks. The unknown person told Krishna that, "these mind tricks are sufficient to make her do all ugly things. After that you will tell Gargi and others that you have several psychological problems because of having a relationship with her. You will also create some social media posts related to that, then you will exit the scene, you and your family are safe".

Now, Vincent plans to turn Aaliyah into a murderer. He thinks that her murder count starts with Krishna. Krishna is the first scapegoat that he is sending to Aaliyah. He will send many after Krishna, to her. He strongly believes that he can turn her into a killing machine by slowly poisoning her mind using Krishna. Vincent had already turned some capable persons to terrorists, and he is expert at this.

Gargi sometimes will call Krishna, she will ask about his job, his family. Krishna will just reply to whatever Gargi asks as instructed. As three months are getting over in another day, the unknown person sends him the flight ticket from Coimbatore to Mumbai. Krishna told his mother and sister that he will have to go back to Mumbai. They are worried that they are going to miss him. His mother asked him whether he can extend the "work from home" option. Krishna said, "No, maximum 3 months can be taken in a year and that I have taken now, I can come next year only". Krishna received a call from Gargi, she asked him, "when will you reach Mumbai?". Krishna replied, "Just now I got my flight tickets". Gargi asked, "'got' your flight tickets?". Krishna said, "actually booked my flight tickets", then he shared the flight details. Gargi asks him to send her a whatsapp message when he reaches Mumbai. Krishna said, "ok".

The next night, his mother and sister's eyes were full of tears. His mother gave him idly powder and other goodies which Krishna likes the most. She advised him not to go out late, and asked him to eat properly, while sending him off in a taxi to the airport. He catches the flight and reaches Mumbai.

As Aaliyah is so busy with her work, she cannot go to Coimbatore to meet him. She was waiting for his arrival. When Krishna reached his apartment. He sent a whatsapp message to Gargi. Gargi replied, "Welcome back Krishna". Gargi informs Aaliyah and Aaliyah plans to meet him. Then after some time, the unknown person called Krishna and said, "Welcome back Krishna, Aaliyah is coming to your house to meet you, you should make her feel weak", he is in the opposite building and able to see part of Krishna's house through a window in Krishna's house. Krishna looked outside through his window while he was speaking with the unknown person, he saw three black Defender cars, then a cherry red Rolls Royce car, then a black Benz s class, two black Land Rover cars on the opposite side of the street. Security persons first surrounded the Rolls Royce car.

The unknown person said "After welcoming her, while you have a conversation with her, suddenly ask her whether she is an orphan" as Aaliyah grew up in a home and she does not have parents. Krishna asked him, "Do I have to use the word orphan?". The unknown person said, "have you forgotten the training? You applied for a job in her company, told Gargi about that and you are working in her company, moreover she is the world's richest person, so naturally she will feel superior when she is with you, do not ask me any questions, do whatever I say, think of your mother and sister". An effective way to attack a person is to use their weakness. Vincent thought that after setting this weakness, he will be able to give continuous pain to her.

A security person opened the door and Aaliyah stepped out of the Rolls Royce. The unknown person commented, "oh! she looks damn hot in her beige silk evening dress". Then she reached Krishna's door, rang the doorbell. The unknown person hung up the call. Krishna wore the headset as instructed and opened the door. Krishna's mind is full of the dark training that he has gone through for the past three months. Krishna asked her to come inside, complimented her about her look, asked to have a seat and he asked whether she likes red wine. Aaliyah said, "ah! Last time you did not compliment me and you did not offer me a drink, you look different". Krishna said, "yes, I have changed my hair style". Krishna did not know when to ask her that question, he was nervous. Aaliyah saw him and asked, "do you miss your mother and sister? Gargi told me about your family". Krishna replied,"Yes I miss them", he thought that it was the right time to shoot out that question, he asked "are you an orphan? ah...I read that on the internet". Now Vincent is smiling as he is also listening to their conversation. Aaliyah replied, "No, I have a mother and a little sister" and she said, "your family is my family". Krishna is not trained for this reply. Aaliyah then said, "I am happy that you joined our company, actually you are also the owner of the company, but you chose to work as an employee". Now, Krishna recalled that whenever she praises, he should immediately speak about her weakness. Krishna said, "you may have yearned for a parent when you were a kid, you may have felt jealous being with kids who actually have parents, how did you overcome that feeling and become successful?". Aaliyah replied, "most orphans do not have access to basic needs and education, may lack social skills, they may even get exploited but I am fortunate that I was brought up by Sister Venessa, a great soul, who lived her whole life caring for others. She made sure that everyone in the home gets proper education, and everyone is loved. I am what I am today because of her". Vincent wants to see the ugly side of Aaliyah very badly. Krishna recalled his training that now he should make her feel that she should not have shared this with him. Krishna asked, "is she alive?". Actually this is Krishna's third attempt. Aaliyah replied, "always, in my heart, she has a permanent place in my heart just like you". Aaliyah came closer to Krishna, his heart was racing, she whispered in his ear, "don't make me wait longer, love you". Krishna said, "love you" firmly, for a second, he forgot that he is wired and his dark training. Aaliyah's eyes lit up, when Krishna confirmed his love in words, Aaliyah kissed him but Krishna did not want to engage in that kiss, he did not open his lips. There are many thoughts running in his mind that he should not make a good relationship with her, when she makes the first move he should mock her, what will happen to her sister since he made a terrible mistake. Aaliyah asked him, "what happened?", still holding his cheeks looking into his eyes, looking to kiss him again, but properly this time. Krishna replied, "I feel nauseous", his fourth attempt. Aaliyah called his security who was standing outside the door and she told him, "call a doctor immediately". Krishna said, "Not needed, I am fine". Aaliyah asked him to sit on the couch and drink some water. Aaliyah looks worried. Krishna told her, "I am fine, I don't need a doctor". Aaliyah said, "I cannot leave you like this. I want to make sure that you are fine". Krishna said, "I am totally fine". Aaliyah asked, "are you sure?". Krishna said, "yes". Aaliyah asked Krishna to take note of her phone number. Krishna noted her phone number. Aaliyah asked Krishna to call her or call Gargi if she is not available for anything, then she asked him to take rest and she left his house.

After Aaliyah left the apartment, Krishna got a call from the unknown person. The unknown person asked, "why did you say that you love her?". Krishna said, "I am sorry".

The unknown person said, "Do you want to have sex with her? Is that more important than your family? Actually our men are following you sister, she is returning to your home from her friend's birthday party. Shall I ask our men to crash the car into her scooter?". Krishna said, "No No please don't do this". Actually Vincent's men are not going to do any harm to Krishna's family, but they will create fear and they will come up with some compelling reason for Krishna to work effectively for them. Now the reason is Krishna told Aaliyah that he loves her. Their target is Aaliyah. The unknown person asked him, "It seemed like she was telling something in your ear, what did she tell?". Krishna repeated the words that she told him, "don't make me wait longer, love you". The unknown person replied, "you lost your sense then...we have to rectify this, we have to create a situation where she gets offended, you should say that you love her at that time in the same way that you told her for the first time". Krishna said, "ok".

Someone might notice that Aaliyah meets Krishna and may spread the news that they are dating. Vincent does not want that to happen since people will think Aaliyah as a "down to earth" person for dating a guy from a middle class family. He wants the world to look at Aaliyah like she is a wild animal. Vincent has connections to all newspaper companies, news channels, and all social media owners. Vincent asked his connections to make sure that this news does not surface on any medium.

The next day Krishna went to office, while entering the office, he noticed that there were posters saying, "Our founder visiting our compass today, she is going to have a one to one meeting with employees chosen randomly. Register by scanning this QR code". The unknown person called Krishna and said, "Aaliyah will choose you even when you do not register, do not register for that". Krishna told him that he will not register for that. Krishna meets his team. The team members were happy to see Krishna. They had the usual standup meeting. Krishna joined his team for the coffee break. Team members were speaking about the one to one meeting with the founder. Some of them told, what they would ask if they were chosen. Then they asked Krishna whether he registered for that. Krishna replied, "yes", thinking he might be chosen as the unknown person said. They asked what he would ask if he was chosen. Krishna replied, "I would ask why we need ID cards, we can implement some machine learning employee identification system that would identify an employee, ID card should become an old school technology". All team members appreciated him very much. His manager told him, "Great idea Krishna, even if you do not get a chance to speak to her today, you can send this suggestion using our internal suggestions website which will reach up to the top most level".

All employees in the company seemed really excited about the one to one meeting. After the coffee break, Krishna and his team went back to their place. While Aaliyah was speaking to the fourth employee. There was an announcement, "Next employee is Krishna from the NLP team, please come to the waiting lounge near the founder's office". As expected, Krishna's name was called. Krishna has put a shocking reaction on his face that his name was called. Team members were very happy and they cheered him. Krishna got a call from the unknown person. Krishna attended the call and fixed one side of the headset in his ear. The unknown person asked him to carry his laptop bag too. Krishna does not want to know why. The unknown person said, "You will find a small gift box inside your laptop bag, which you have to give it to her before you leave the room". Krishna said "ok". The unknown person said, "as you told her that you love her yesterday, you will have to speak nicely for a minute, then we will give you a signal, your cell phone will vibrate continuously for 2 seconds, that time you have to speak about her weakness". Krishna asks, "about being an orphan?". The unknown person said, "yes, otherwise speak about her friends circle, she has only one friend Gargi, tell her that Gargi told you about this", then said "you will get another signal to leave, say something and leave from her room". Krishna asked him "what's inside the gift box". The unknown person said, "There is a necklace with a dollar, in that dollar, a text 'Aaliyah Krishna' is written which has Krishna as last name, an indirect cue which would remind her that she is an orphan. There is also a paper inside the gift box with text 'I LOVE YOU'". This is the rectification that the unknown person told to Krishna. He reached the office, he was breathing deeply, waiting to be called inside.

After a few minutes, as the fourth employee left Aaliyah's room, a person at the desk in the lounge asked Krishna to enter the room. Krishna entered the room. Aaliyah was standing near her table. Aaliyah asked, "are you ok now?". Krishna replied, "yes, I am fine now". Aaliyah said, "Come sit here", showing him the chair in the room. Krishna sat in that chair. Aaliyah said, "I want to meet you at least once in a day. I created this event, just to talk with you for some time, people will start to gossip if I meet you often, I do not know how I am going to meet you every day". As instructed Krishna replied, "I was eagerly waiting for my name to be announced". Aaliyah laughed and Krishna also started laughing with her. Then Krishna received the signal, his cell phone was vibrating. Krishna said, "But you should never use the company like this, I thought you were worshiping the company like a temple". Aaliyah replied, "I would do anything to meet you or speak with you even if the price is my life". Krishna said, "I think you are thinking in this way because you do not have a bigger circle of friends, Gargi told me that she is the only friend that you have". Aaliyah said, "Krishna, how about drawing a smaller circle around us and not letting anyone inside". Immediately, Krishna started to cough, Aaliyah then grabbed a paper cup. Instead of pressing the normal water button, she pressed the hot water button, she was also looking at Krishna whether he is ok. The hot water actually spilled in her hand, immediately she dropped the cup on the floor. Krishna saw that, he ran to her, he held her hand like people would carry blessed food in a temple. He asked her, "are you okay?", looking at her hand with his eyes wide open to make sure that she was not wounded and he blew some air over her hand. She said, "I'm ok". Then he got the second signal from the unknown person. Krishna then took the gift out of his bag and gave it to Aaliyah. Aaliyah said, "Thank you". Krishna then asked, "can I leave If there is nothing else". Aaliyah said, "yes, we will meet again very soon".

After some time, he got a call from the unknown person. The unknown person asked him sarcastically, "Is she okay?". Krishna replied, "actually hot water got spilled on her hand". The unknown person then asked him, "Do I want to remind you about your family every time? It is difficult to create pain for her for the first time, but once that is done, then it will be a piece of cake to create more pain. One time is enough, be serious, focus only on your goal, do not react to your impulses". Krishna said, "I will not miss the next chance", not knowing what to tell him.

The unknown person said, "You should have done it by now. You don't have to give her the gift". Krishna said, "I gave the gift to her". The unknown person asked, "what? All that training which we gave you is a waste? You should do anything to her only as a token of mercy or to show her that you are superior to her". Krishna apologized to him again. The unknown person then told him to wait for their signal before he does anything so that this mistake never happens again.

Krishna does not want to continue with this anymore. Krishna wants to end this sooner. Then suddenly the things which he spoke in the coffee break came to his mind, he did not speak about that. Krishna opened the internal suggestions site in his mobile phone. He typed his idea and submitted it. Krishna went back to his team. His team members asked him what he spoke with Aaliyah. Krishna told them that he told Aaliyah whatever they discussed in their coffee break. Team members were curious about the reply he got from her. He told them that she actually likes that idea and told me that she will think about it.

Once Aaliyah is done speaking with everyone. Once she got free, she tore the gift wrapper and opened the gift box. Then Aaliyah sent a message to Krishna, "I LOVE YOU". The unknown person asked Krishna to react with love emoji immediately which Krishna did.

Krishna's manager asked Krishna whether he could speak 5 minutes with him. Krishna thought about the manager meeting in his last company. He went with his manager, and his manager said, "we are impressed with your performance, the top-level management has decided to switch you to a different project". Krishna told his manager, "I really like this team and project". Then his manager advised him, "see this could be a big opportunity, you should seize this opportunity, you can interact with our team if you work in a different team and you can help the team if the team needs your help". Then the manager also said, "whenever the team plans any outing, we will include you as well". Krishna finally accepted to change to a different team. Vincent has no idea about what Aaliyah was planning about Krishna.

The next day, Aaliyah arranged a "suggestion appreciation" meeting for the whole company in the morning. Everyone including Krishna went to attend the meeting in the big meeting hall. Aaliyah welcomed everyone and said, "one of our employees has provided an excellent suggestion, pointing out that we are still using an old way of doing a basic thing, and we are not utilizing the advanced technology. The employee's suggestion is to use ourselves as an ID instead of using an ID card. Nowadays, even smartphones use face ID to authenticate, then why do we still use ID cards?". Then she said, "I want to welcome Krishna from the NLP team on stage please, one who provided this suggestion". Everyone was applauding for his idea.

Krishna got really happy and he went to the stage. She saw him, this is enough for Aaliyah to get through that day. Then Aaliyah said, "we will have to implement this feature in our company, for that we have to create a separate team, Krishna will be promoted as project head and he will be leading the entire team". Krishna cannot believe what he has heard, his eyebrow reached the top of his head. Then Aaliyah said, "yes Krishna's hierarchy is changed and he will be reporting directly to me". All employees in the meeting hall were stunned hearing that, murmuring "from developer to Project head!". She gave him a "Best suggestion" shield, then she shook Krishna's hand and she squeezed his palm as a way to say that she cannot wait to grab him.

The meeting got over, everyone went back to their places discussing Krishna's humongous achievement. Krishna went to his place. Everyone in the team appreciated him, they saw his shield. Everyone started to take pictures with him and with his shield. They asked him for a big treat for his achievement. Krishna asked them to plan the treat. Then Krishna opened his laptop, he received an email from HR regarding his promotion details. His current salary is 15 lakhs per annum and his new salary is 2 crore per annum plus stock shares, his eyes were about to jump out. Then he got a meeting invite from Aaliyah that is scheduled on the next day to discuss the new project.

Krishna's manager arranged a send off meeting for Krishna, although Krishna is not relieving from the company, he is just switching the team. Krishna has worked almost 4 months on this project. The team members shared what they felt working with him. Krishna also shared his thoughts about them.

Vincent did not expect this. He thought that switching Krishna to Aaliyah's company was a mistake. His initial thought was he must place Krishna as close as possible to Aaliyah to achieve whatever he is planning. Maybe Krishna's caring towards her might have made her take this decision, a costly mistake. If Krishna is asked to reject this offer, then he will appear like a fool in her company. If Krishna is made to resign from his job, then it will be like he is moving away from Aaliyah altogether. Now that Aaliyah has done something big for Krishna and she loves him more, It's time to make Krishna appear more evil to Aaliyah, but before that Krishna must receive a bigger reward than what Aaliyah gave him. Krishna must look more powerful than Aaliyah in some way and that will bring out the evil in her.

Krishna was so happy, that night, he called his mother and told her that he was promoted as project head. His mother and his sister were happy about him. His mother asked him whether she can start looking for an alliance for him. Krishna knows that he cannot look for alliance until he is done with Aaliyah as instructed to him in his dark training. Krishna asked his mother to wait for another 1 year, until his sister finishes the B.Tech course. His mother told him that, as it will take time for finding a good alliance, she will start looking for alliances and she will be able to find one within this 1 year time. But Krishna asked her to wait another year, he told her that he will marry when he is 28. His mother asked him whether he is in love with anyone. Krishna replied, "No". Then he spoke to his sister. His sister said, "you have created all social media accounts which you don't like. You can tell me about my sister-in-law, I won't tell mom". Krishna told her that there is no one.

The unknown person called Krishna. Krishna attended the call. The unknown person told Krishna that he had installed an online rummy app in Krishna's phone. He asked Krishna to open the app and login with the login details that he has sent him. Krishna logged in. The unknown person asked him to open account details in the app which he did. Krishna cannot even read the amount in words that is displayed as the amount that he has won. It's 15 and seven zeroes, that means it is 15 crores. The unknown person told Krishna that he should tell Aaliyah and everyone that he has won 15 crores by playing rummy in this app. Krishna is speechless, 15 crores in a second! Vincent is ready to do anything to win over Aaliyah. The unknown person told Krishna that he should not spend this money until they ask him to do so and he asked him to go to Martin car showroom and book a car.

Krishna reached the car showroom, where every document was made ready. The unknown person called Krishna and told him that he just had to sign those documents. Krishna did as instructed. The car will be available after 2 days. Actually Vincent's plan is to make Krishna tell Aaliyah that he has booked a car for her in return for promoting him as a project head. Krishna will not let Aaliyah know the model and colour he booked until he actually presents the car. Aaliyah already had the same model with the same color, but she sold at a very cheap price not even half the price of the car because she met with a minor accident due to brake failure. The news has become viral because she sold a new car with such a cheap price tag. Once Krishna tells Aaliya about the booking of a luxury car, it will make Aaliyah think that Krishna is trying to be superior over her. Then, it will be the right time to apply an evil mask to Krishna. Krishna will show Aaliyah, what model and colour that he actually booked. This will set the seed for evilness deep inside her. Once that is done, then watering it everyday will be an easy task.

The next day, before Krishna reaches office, the unknown person called him and told him that he needs to tell all his previous teammates and also Aaliya that he has won 15 crores in the online rummy game. After Krishna reaches the office, he goes and meets the old teammates and tells them about the money. His teammates were discussing how lucky he is to receive another huge reward. Krishna has to attend the meeting that Aaliyah has scheduled to discuss about the new project. Aaliyah reached the meeting room 5 minutes before Krishna. Krishna reached the meeting room on time. Aaliyah said,

"Ah! finally", feeling happy that she got today's dose to extend her life for another day. Aaliyah extended her hand to shake Krishna's hand. Krishna gave his hand. While shaking Krishna's hand, for a split second, she thought she could just pull him towards her, but she will not do that in the workplace. Then Aaliyah asked, "you seem really excited for the new role" and said "you will get another promotion too". Krishna asked, "What's that?". Aaliyah said, "CEO of the company". They were laughing. Krishna said, "actually I have won 15 crores in an online rummy app". Aaliyah said, "oh really! Congrats Krishna! You must be really lucky". Krishna said, "Thanks, I have booked a luxury car for you which you have to accept". Aaliyah replied, "I will accept whatever you buy me, how will I not accept anything that Krishna buys for me, it is precious than anything else". Krishna was instructed to deliver a dialogue with a self boasting facial expression which he does without any mistake, "You will be impressed by my gift". Vincent listening to their conversation was thinking about the pain that she is going to experience. Aaliyah said, "you are my gift". Then they were discussing the project implementation. Krishna told her that he would need a team with one manager, one lead, two senior and four junior developers and needed to take 360 degree photos of all employees in the company. Aaliyah told him that she will make arrangements for it.

Once he left the meeting room, the unknown person called him and asked him, "did you keep the same facial expression?". Krishna said, "yes". The unknown person said, "good". They want to encourage him to make him work effectively. After Krishna reached home, that night, he called his mother, told that he received 15 crore money in an online rummy app. His mother asked him, "how can they pay that much amount? Are you involved in any criminal activity?". Krishna said, "it is a kind of gambling". Then his mother said, "Don't play gambling games, first you win some money then you will lose all your money, also you may be arrested for playing those games". In order to pacify his mother Krishna told, "No it is not gambling, it is just a game". Mother asked him, "how can they pay you such a huge amount". Krishna told, "I played many times, each time I won some amount". His mother asked him to stop playing those games. Then he spoke to his sister. His sister told him that she will explain to their mother. His sister and mother were so happy that their family got settled and there will not be any financial problems in their life.

The next day when Krishna reaches the office, Krishna sees a meeting invitation email, scheduled with him and other 8 employees. All those 8 employees are very soft spoken, Aaliyah wants to make Krishna as comfortable as possible. As yesterday, Aaliyah reached 5 minutes before the meeting. Krishna got a call from the unknown person, asking him to meet Aaliyah before the meeting begins. Vincent wants Krishna to be nice with Aaliyah now before she sees his evil nature that day night as the car will be delivered that day night. Krishna reached the meeting immediately by running. Aaliyah saw Krishna enter the meeting room and catch his breath. Krishna was looking sexy and she got turned on, then she thought that she cannot lose control in her workplace. Aaliyah's face turned red and her voice was a little shaky while she asked him to take the seat. She closed her eyes for a few seconds, then she became normal. Then other employees began to enter the meeting room. She started the meeting, she said that the company is planning to implement a new feature and

Krishna is their project head. She explained the hierarchies. After that she asked Krishna to take it forward and she left.

That day night when Krishna reached his house. The unknown person called him and asked Krishna to call Aaliyah and ask her whether he can meet Aaliyah today in her house to give her the gift. Krishna called her and asked her. Aaliyah said they can meet. The unknown person called him again and said, "you are going to give her the car today". First he will give her the car key like one would give a wedding ring. The car key will be placed inside a gift box of the same type which he gave already. Then he will receive a signal, that time he needs to hug her and whisper the words "ride safely" in her ear the same way she whispered in his ear when she met him in his house. Actually those words have double meanings. Then he has to tell her that the car delivery truck will arrive soon and he should leave her house.

That night Krishna reached Aaliyah's house. The main gate security made a phone call and the security asked Krishna to enter the house with due respect. Krishna had never seen such a big house, he had to travel almost a three fourth of a kilometer in the taxi to reach the main door, there was security every 50 meters. Aaliyah was waiting to receive Krishna. He asked the taxi driver to wait there and he stepped out. He was instructed not to get astonished. Krishna tried to look casual. Then Aaliyah grabbed his hand and took him inside. The house is full of laborers. One is watering the plants, one is cleaning the floor, one is cleaning the glass etc and there were securities with AK 47. The house is pristine, air conditioned, which he cannot even imagine. Krishna said, "Your house is pristine, neat". Aaliyah replied, "just like you". Then Aaliyah asked Krishna, "do you want to see my room". Aaliyah grabbed his hand again and took him inside her room.

Her room looked very simple. There was a double cot bed, a small home office setup which included a table, a chair, a monitor, a laptop, a mouse, a note and pen, then a big buddha statue almost 8 feets tall and 4 feets wide which was lit in a peaceful way. Krishna was looking at the statue for a long time. Aaliyah asked, "you came here to gawk at the statue?". Then Krishna suddenly came to his knees. Aaliyah kept her hand in her mouth in amazement. Then he gave the gift box. Aaliyah replied, "that is very sweet of you". While standing up, he got the signal as instructed, he slipped because of his new shoes. Aaliyah immediately secured him from falling, before he even finished telling the words "Thank you", She locked her lips with his. Then she started unbuttoning his shirt, but he stopped her, telling her that he cannot do that before marriage. Then he told her "ride safely". She started laughing. Krishna cannot understand why she was laughing. She told him, "I don't use safety when I am with you". Again Krishna cannot get what she was saying. Krishna said, "your car delivery truck will arrive soon". Aaliyah couldn't control her laughter, she was laughing out loud hearing the word "delivery". Then she controlled her laughter. Krishna looked exhausted and said that he wants to leave. Aaliyah again grabbed his hand, took him to his taxi. She said that they will meet tomorrow in the office. After some time, the car is delivered to her.

Krishna told the unknown person what exactly happened in her house. The unknown person said, "the price of the car is 5 crores, do you know the value of that amount? Don't you know what is meant by ride in sex?". After mentioning the word sex, Krishna understood what Aaliyah told him. Then the unknown person said, "one more mistake, then your sister will ride many men, do you understand?". Krishna does not want to reply to that. The unknown person asked, "I need a reply. Say yes or no". Krishna said, "yes" after a second.

They taught Krishna every expression, every word that he will speak, the modulation he has to use, the way he should walk but they failed this time. It is like creating a humanoid robot and expecting a perfect behaviour. It is difficult to preprogram every use case. But Vincent will even take 1000 more attempts and he does not want to lose.

The next day, Krishna reached office, he saw an email from Aaliyah. In that email it was mentioned that she has created a website for employees to book their time slot for 360 degree photography. Each time slot is 10 minutes. She has also arranged a room for taking 360 degree photography, she has invited a third party photography team and they will cooperate as per Krishna's needs. Whenever any employee books a timeslot, their details will automatically get added to Krishna's calendar as an event. Krishna opened his calendar. The first event is with an employee with id "000001", name "Aaliyah", the founder and CEO of the company.

He then reaches the room that is arranged for 360 degree photography. He receives a call from the unknown person. Krishna does not want to attend the call, but he attended it. The unknown person said, "while taking photos of Aaliyah, you have to tell her some corrections continuously to the point where she gets frustrated like you got frustrated while attending this call, you have to continue doing that even if it takes an hour or two". Krishna said, "ok". Then the photography team arrived, they were setting up all the lighting and cameras. He met his team. Then after some time, Aaliyah reaches the room, as per her schedule. She finds Krishna as soon as she enters the room.

Krishna asked her to stand on the mini stage for a 360 degree photo. She stood there. Photography team started taking photos as per Krishna's instructions.

Krishna started telling her corrections. Krishna was saying, "chin up...no little down..no little up...actually you closed your eyes...you are leaning forward...you have to stand straight...now turn to left...little more...no not that much". After a few minutes, his team members got scared when Krishna was telling her more corrections. Then the manager in Krishna's team went up to him and told him that it will land them in trouble if he continues doing that as Aaliyah is the founder of the company in an ascii voice. Aaliyah can see what they are talking about. She was enjoying every second and whenever Krishna tells her any correction, the real camera for her is Krishna's eyes, she always looks right in that camera. Aaliyah asked her assistant to cancel all the meetings, however important they may be, until she is finished with the photography before entering the room. Then Aaliyah started making mistakes on purpose. He asked to wear the face mask, she wore it without covering the nose, he asked her to cover the nose also. Then he asked to wear a spectacle, Aaliyah turned the spectacle upside down and wore it, Krishna said, "your spectacle is upside down", then she wore it correctly. Krishna's team members cannot understand why Aaliyah is making these mistakes. Then Krishna got a signal as instructed, he said to Aaliyah that photography is completed. Then Aaliyah left the room.

Vincent was hoping that this would anger Aaliyah but it did not. So he came up with another plan. The most effective technique to set the evil seed inside Aaliyah would be to damage someone in her mind, to whom she has much respect and love. He thought he could use Sister Venessa.

That night, the unknown person called Krishna and told him that he must speak ill of Sister Venessa, asked Krishna to call Aaliyah for dinner, then while having some conversation, he should say these words, "Nuns are great, as they do not live for themselves, yearn for nothing, they don't even have sex, but I have heard some stories that nuns may have sex with fathers of the church". Then he told Krishna, "whatever she replies, you have to say", "Even your caregiver Sister Venessa would have been involved in those activities", "with a mocking smile on your face". If Aaliyah ignores, then damage will be less, but if she tries to defend, she will be the rat in the cage. Then Sister Venessa can be damaged again and again, even with indirect cues, ultimately turning her into a monster. Vincent thought this should definitely work as Krishna is not giving any indirect cues for her, he is going to speak directly. As Aaliyah loves Krishna more, as she is in hope of getting a family, she will get more pain.

The unknown person also told Krishna that someone will deliver a gift box to him, a small buddha statue. As Aaliyah laughed at Krishna in her house, if Krishna gives this gift after delivering all the dialogues, it would anger Aaliyah more, she would even kill Krishna the minute she sees the buddha. The unknown person asked Krishna to give this gift to Aaliyah after finishing dinner and before she leaves. After some time, Krishna received the gift box. Krishna called Aaliyah and asked her whether they could meet for the dinner. Aaliyah told him that she is free and she suggested a restaurant which she likes. Krishna accepted that. Aaliyah also told him that she would send a car to his apartment. As Krishna always speaks through his headset, looks at his phone for any messages from the unknown person, as he will also be listening to the call, he sees one message from the unknown person "NO", then another message "taxi". Then Krishna told Aaliyah that he would hire a taxi.

Then Krishna reaches the restaurant a little late as instructed. Aaliyah was waiting in front of the restaurant to see Krishna. As Krishna came out of the taxi. Aaliyah went up to him, said hi, then she grabbed his hand, like a mother would grab her 2 year old kid's hand, she will even be happy if he calls her as "mom", Krishna just walks along with her. They went to their reserved table. Aaliyah was speaking about the restaurants, the food she likes in there. Then they were speaking about their early life. Krishna told her that he studied in a christian school. Aaliyah asked him, "have you gone to church for prayers? I love going to church, I have great respect for people who live their life as a service". Krishna received a signal to deliver his first dialogue. Krishna said, "Nuns are great, as they do not live for themselves, yearn for nothing, they don't even have sex, but I have heard some stories that nuns may have sex with fathers of the church". Aaliyah said, "I don't think so". Vincent was happy as she had started defending. Krishna received the second signal. When Krishna started delivering the second dialogue, Aaliyah asked Krishna what they could order for dessert.   Krishna told her, "Ice cream". Aaliyah called the waiter, then Aaliyah asked Krishna what flavour he wanted. The waiter listed the flavours they have "vanilla, strawberry, chocolate, butterscotch, mango". Krishna said, "strawberry". Then Aaliyah told the waiter, "two strawberry ice creams". Then Aaliyah asked, "you were about to say something". Krishna said, "Even your caregiver Sister vanilla would have been involved in those activities". He said vanilla instead of Venessa, then he forgot the name. Aaliyah started laughing and Krishna also started laughing. After finishing with their ice creams, they came out. Aaliyah saw that Krishna was carrying something in his pocket. Aaliyah asked, "what's in your pocket". Krishna did not receive the third signal, so he does not want to give the gift box. But Aaliyah persisted, so Krishna gave her the gift. Aaliyah looked amazed and curious. She opened the gift immediately, "a buddha statue, I love buddha". She hugged him tightly, she did not want to let him go, she would even hug him for her entire life. Then Krishna took his taxi and Aaliyah went to her home.

Vincent cannot use Krishna for this task. Also, he will not create any harm to Krishna or to his family, because Krishna may not do the task if any harm happened to him or his family, and also Aaliyah would know that someone did it to Krishna or his family. More importantly, Aaliyah will start to show more kindness towards Krishna but Krishna should be the one to show kindness to the wounded Aaliyah. He can only make him fear. The unknown person called him and as usual, he scolded for his mistake and made sure he won't do any in future.

The next day, Krishna went to his office. Opened his laptop, then he saw an email from Aaliyah, a meeting invitation. Krishna met her. Aaliyah asked about the progress of the human ID feature. Krishna told her that he has every piece, he just has to connect every piece. He told her that he will complete it in another three days. Vincent has no idea of what to do next, as he has used everything. After three days, Krishna showed her the successful demonstration of the feature. Aaliyah was so happy about it. It worked perfectly.

Then in that evening, Aaliyah scheduled a meeting for the entire company. Aaliyah welcomed everyone and told them, "I have taken a big decision. I am stepping down from the CEO position.". The whole crowd started murmuring, they were discussing who could be their new CEO. After a gap, Aaliyah told them, "The Project head of the Human ID team, Krishna will be our new CEO". Then she called Krishna on stage. She told her employees that she is happy that Krishna has suggested a great idea and he has also implemented that feature within a week's time. She also told them that she hopes that Krishna will bring many new ideas to the company. She congratulated him. After the meeting, while walking his way to the CEO office, everyone congratulated him. His previous team members met him and were very excited about his growth. Then His Human ID team met him. Then Aaliyah met him and asked him to go to his native and take a small break, which Krishna accepted.

That night Krishna called his mother and told her that he is coming home and he said that he has a big surprise, which he will tell her after reaching home. His mother told him, they too have a big surprise, that they will tell him once he reaches home. Krishna cannot think of anything. Krishna boarded the flight. Krishna was thinking hard of what could be that surprise. Then he reached his home. He rang the doorbell. The one who opened the door is not his mother or his sister but it is Aaliyah. She reached his house 4 hours before him. She met his mother and she told her that she loves Krishna. Krishna's mother and sister also like her very much. Then Aaliyah asked Krishna to take her to the terrace.

Krishna took her to the terrace. Krishna could see some black cat securities around the house. Aaliyah said, "I know everything that you went through from the time you joined our company, I know the creepy guy who always calls you, and I also know the man behind him". Krishna was curious, "who is that? I want to know about him". Aaliyah told him, "you don't have to". Krishna was furious, "How can I not know the one who did this to me and you?". Aaliyah asked him, "What are you going to do knowing that?". Krishna said, "punish him, put him under bars". Aaliyah smiled and said, "The feeling that he cannot finish what he started will kill him". Krishna looked so beautiful when he was angry. Aaliyah cannot resist the urge to kiss him. She kissed him immediately. Aaliyah could have saved Krishna and his family when she got to know about this but if she had done that, Krishna would not have agreed to marry her. Also, Aaliyah knows that Vincent will not harm them. Actually Aaliyah used Vincent to get Krishna.

Then they announced their marriage to the world. Many of them attended their marriage including Gargi. His previous team members were discussing that he joined as a developer, then he got promoted as project head, then he got promoted as CEO, then he finally married the founder of the company, in between he also won 15 crores in an online rummy game.